W9-BPK-161

CHAPPAQUA LIBRARY,
CHAPPAQUA, N. Y.

CHAPPAQUA LIBRARY,
CHAPPAQUA, N. Y.

Gandhi

Gandhi

LEONARD EVERETT FISHER

Atheneum Books for Young Readers

CHAPPAQUA LIBRARY
CHAPPAQUA N.Y.

CHRONOLOGY OF MOHANDAS KARAMCHAND GANDHI (1869–1948)

1869	Born in Porbandar, India
1882	Marries Kasturbai Makanji
1887	First son, Harilal, is born
1888–1891	Studies law in England
1891	Returns to India
	Second son, Manilal, is born
1893–1915	Lives in South Africa
1896	Third son, Ramdas, is born
1899	Fourth son, Devadas, is born
1908	Gives up law practice in South Africa
1910	Establishes Tolstoy Farm
1915	Returns to India
1915–1920	Becomes India's political leader
1919	Amristar massacre
1922–1924	Imprisoned for anti-British writings
1930	Arrested without being charged
	Leads the Salt March
1932	Fasts to protest British colonial rule
1942–1944	Jailed as head of campaign for
	Indian independence
1944	Kasturbai dies
1946	Great Britain offers India independence
1947	India becomes independent
1947–1948	Hindu–Muslim Partition riots
1948	Assassinated in Delhi

Copyright © 1995 by Leonard Everett Fisher
Atheneum Books for Young Readers
An imprint of Simon & Schuster Children's Publishing Division
1230 Avenue of the Americas, New York, NY 10020
All rights reserved including the right of
reproduction in whole or in part in any form.
Designed by Carolyn Boschi
The text of this book is set in 14 point Weiss.
The illustrations were done in acrylic paints on paper.
Library of Congress Catalog Card Number: 95-77023
ISBN: 0-689-80337-0
Printed in the United States of America
First edition
10 9 8 7 6 5 4 3 2 1

With appreciation to Professor Richard Fox

PUNJAB

• Amritsar

Delhi •
◆ New Delhi

PAKISTAN

INDIA

PAKISTAN

Persian Gulf

Gulf of Oman

• Rajkot

Dandi

Porbandar

Arabian Peninsula

Bay of
Bengal

OMAN

Bombay

YEMEN

Arabian Sea

Red Sea

CEYLON

AFRICA

BRITISH
SOMALILAND

THE INDIAN OCEAN AREA
1948

KENYA

For my grandson,
Jordan Lucas,
with love

ZANZIBAR

TANGANYIKA

MOZAMBIQUE

MADAGASCAR

INDIAN OCEAN

Pretoria
Johannesburg

SOUTH
AFRICA

NATAL

• Durban

1 inch on the map = 620 miles or 1033 kilometers

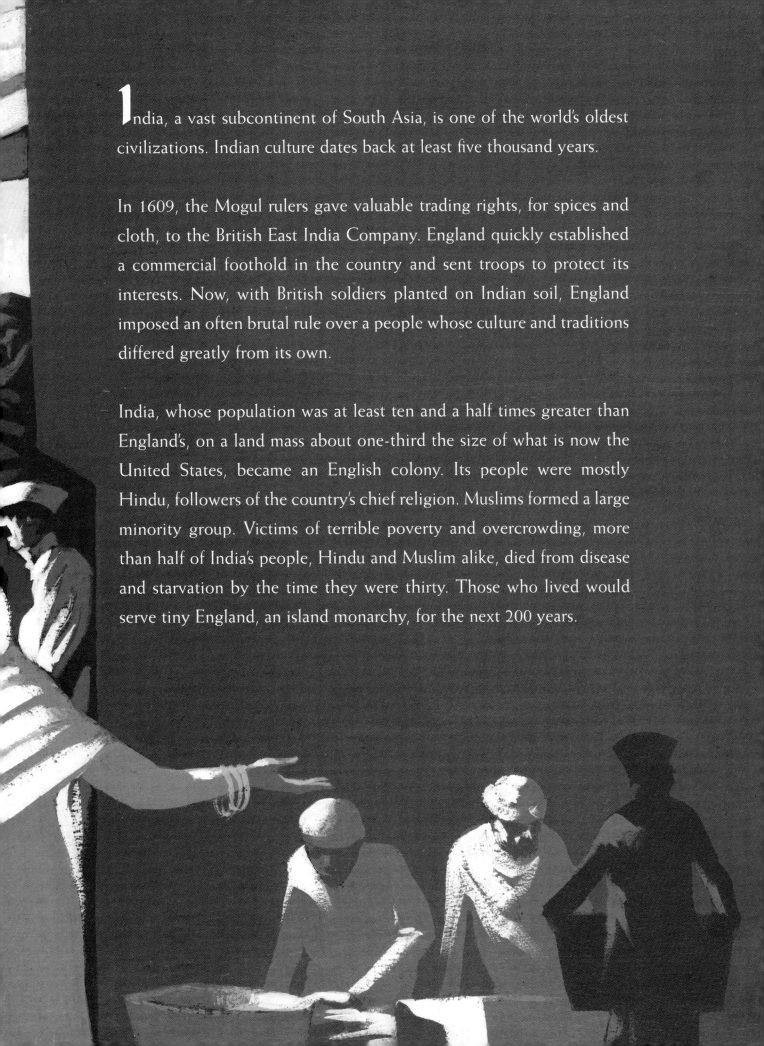

India, a vast subcontinent of South Asia, is one of the world's oldest civilizations. Indian culture dates back at least five thousand years.

In 1609, the Mogul rulers gave valuable trading rights, for spices and cloth, to the British East India Company. England quickly established a commercial foothold in the country and sent troops to protect its interests. Now, with British soldiers planted on Indian soil, England imposed an often brutal rule over a people whose culture and traditions differed greatly from its own.

India, whose population was at least ten and a half times greater than England's, on a land mass about one-third the size of what is now the United States, became an English colony. Its people were mostly Hindu, followers of the country's chief religion. Muslims formed a large minority group. Victims of terrible poverty and overcrowding, more than half of India's people, Hindu and Muslim alike, died from disease and starvation by the time they were thirty. Those who lived would serve tiny England, an island monarchy, for the next 200 years.

Seventy thousand people lived in ancient Porbandar, a small city on India's west coast, when Mohandas Karamchand Gandhi was born there on October 2, 1869. He was the youngest of six children.

His father, Karamchand, or "Kaba," Gandhi, was a Hindu and three times a widower. He was a skilled but underpaid diplomat and struggled to make ends meet. Kaba Gandhi worked as minister to the British for the maharaja of Porbandar. The very wealthy maharaja ran the town, but only because the British let him. Kaba kept the British at bay and the maharaja on his throne. Mohandas's mother, Putlibai, was a devout Hindu who prayed and fasted continuously.

Kaba and Putlibai Gandhi, together with Kaba's five brothers, their wives, and numerous children and grandchildren, lived crowded together in a three-story house. When Mohandas was seven years old, Kaba moved his entire family east to Rajkot. As minister to the maharaja there, he was jailed by the British for defending the prince against British insults. His father's politics and his mother's religious beliefs were important influences on young Gandhi.

By the time Mohandas was thirteen years old, he was married off to Kasturbai Makanji, who was the same age. The two teenagers hardly knew each other. According to custom, their parents had arranged for the wedding. The marriage, however, lasted for sixty-two years, and through four sons. In 1944 Kasturbai died in a British prison in India. She had been jailed for protesting colonial rule.

At nineteen, Mohandas was shipped off to London, England, to attend law school. His family had scraped together all their money in the hope that Mohandas, as a British-educated lawyer, would bring them position and wealth.

Kasturbai and their year-old son, Harilal, were left behind. During the first months that Mohandas studied English law, he quit looking and behaving like the person he was—an Indian Hindu. He became a fashionable British gentleman. Instead of wearing an Indian turban and loose-fitting garments, he sported well-tailored suits laced with a gold chain, stiff-collared shirts, ties, polished shoes, and a top hat. He took dancing and violin lessons and went to parties carrying a silver-headed walking stick. But shy Mohandas remained uncomfortable among fashionable British party-goers. Besides, the fancy clothes cost too much. Mohandas gave up his stylish appearance and set the pattern for his life. He decided to value his mind more than fashion and money.

Mohandas went home in 1891 with a British law degree. He began practicing in Bombay, the country's largest city, seventy-five miles south of Porbandar. But his only clients were too poor to pay him. His shyness was so intense that Mohandas could hardly talk in front of Bombay judges and juries. His family had spent its savings trying to make him a success, and Mohandas was turning into a failure.

Worse still, young Gandhi was thrown bodily out of a British official's house when he sought help for one of his brothers. The official, who had been a party-going friend in London, accused Gandhi of trading on their friendship. Gandhi denied the accusation and threatened to sue the man, but never did. The episode unnerved Gandhi. He felt he had been treated rudely in his own country by an arrogant British official who did not belong there in the first place. Swallowing his pride, Gandhi resolved to find a better life.

An opportunity came in 1893. Gandhi was asked to represent an Indian company in a civil suit in South Africa, another British colony. Gandhi jumped at the chance. He left India for the city of Durban in the province of Natal, the center of Indian culture in South Africa. He was to be gone a year.

After working for several weeks in Durban, Gandhi bought a first-class seat on a train to Pretoria, where the case would be heard. That night he was kicked off the train for refusing to sit in the baggage car. The conductor said that "sammies"—an insulting South African term for the brown-skinned people of India—belonged in the baggage car. That was the law as set down by the white Englishmen and Boers who ran the country. The Boers were farmers, descendants of early Dutch settlers of the region.

Gandhi quickly learned that the Indian people were treated more unjustly in colonial South Africa than they were in colonial India. Gandhi arrived in Pretoria by stagecoach, after having been forced to sit outside the carriage on the coachman's footboard, next to the driver. Outraged by the experience, he resolved to fight back, legally. Overcoming his natural shyness, Gandhi sued the railroad that had denied him his rightful seat, and won a grudging victory! The law was changed so that all Indians could sit in the seat to which their tickets entitled them—provided they wore English-style clothing. Word of this victory spread quickly, and Gandhi soon became a champion of Indian rights in South Africa and, indirectly, a spokesman for all the powerless nonwhites there.

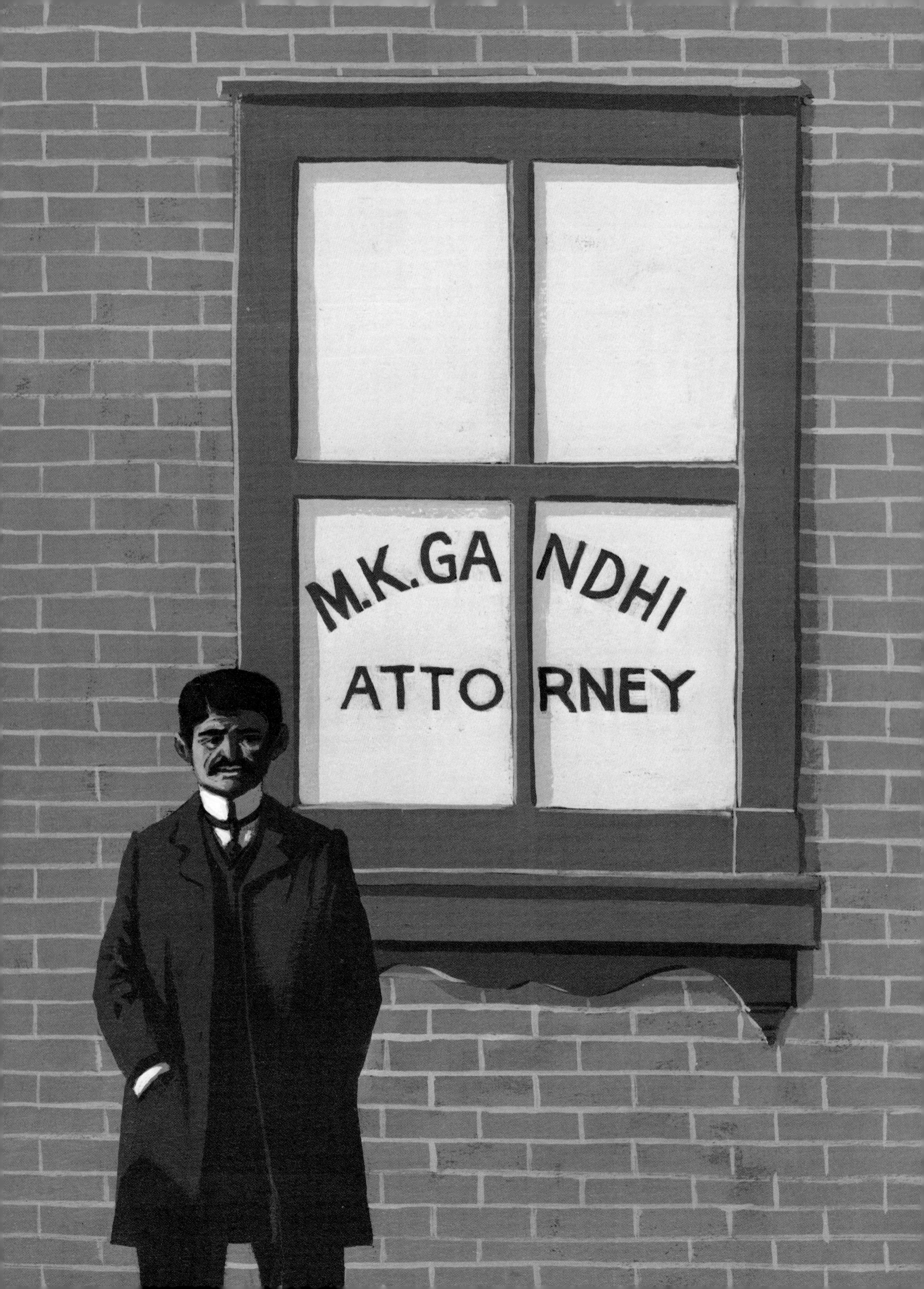
M.K.GANDHI
ATTORNEY

Gandhi's first year in South Africa ended. The case for which he had been hired was settled. But he did not return to India immediately. His court victory had energized him, and he remained to fight against the discrimination of South African citizens of Indian ancestry.

Life in South Africa was becoming harsher for Indians and blacks alike. Either one, for example, could be arrested for walking on the same sidewalk as whites. But in 1894, blacks, even though they outnumbered both whites and Indians in South Africa, were not seen as a threat to whites. They had neither the education nor the growing wealth of the Indians.

South Africa tried to stop Indian immigration. Natal lawmakers wanted to deny the Indian minority the right to vote. They hoped to make life so unbearable for Indians that they would return to India. If the Indians did not leave, they would, in effect, be enslaved by repressive South African laws.

Successful South African Indians were not about to have their status reduced. Gandhi took up their cause. He held meetings and rallies and made plans to resist the enemies of Indian citizens of the British Empire through the courts and without violence.

"In a nonviolent conflict," he would later explain, "there is no rancor left behind and, in the end, the enemies are converted to friends."

In time, Gandhi's calm but vigorous protests against the "no vote for Indians" bill became international news. The British Colonial Office, pressured by world opinion, said that every citizen of the British Empire had the right to vote and to emigrate anywhere in the empire. The British also said that it was illegal to prevent citizens from exercising their rights. Gandhi had won again! But only briefly. South Africa's white lawmakers overruled the Colonial Office and passed the bill.

Gandhi was frustrated but quietly defiant. He would remain in South Africa with his wife and, by 1899, four sons, for another twenty years, struggling for Indian justice. During that period he founded the Natal Indian Congress, a political organization whose sole purpose was to win equal rights for South Africa's Indians. Now a symbol of minority injustice, Gandhi won the respect of England and the world and was hailed as a hero in India. Still, he was beaten by mobs in South Africa, against whom he refused to press charges.

"My notion of democracy," he would write, "is that under it the weakest should have the same opportunity as the strongest."

Between 1899 and 1902 the Boers fought the British in a bloody attempt to carve their own independent state out of two South African provinces. Gandhi remained loyal to England. Serving in uniform with a noncombatant medical unit, he was decorated by the victorious British for his part in the Boer War.

Gandhi continued his fight for Indian civil rights, but by 1904, the white-controlled government had still not righted the wrongs against the Indians of South Africa. He continued to sue the government for its injustices while personally caring for the poor and sick of every color.

In 1906, the Zulu people of Natal rebelled. Again, Gandhi, loyal to Great Britain, served in a military medical unit. But Zulu spears proved no match for the British infantry. Warriors taken prisoner were brutally flogged. Many died. Appalled at the violence, Gandhi vowed to continue using nonviolent means in his own political fight.

Between 1907 and 1914, Gandhi and his followers, the Satyagrahis—"insisters on truth and love"—were repeatedly jailed as they peacefully refused to submit to unjust laws. By 1914, more than one hundred thousand Indians were either in jail or on strike.

Annoyed with white bigotry, Gandhi returned to the plain, loose-fitting wraparound garments of his Hindu heritage. His clothing became both a symbol of his defiance of white culture and an image that brought him closer to his own people.

The whole world criticized the unyielding policies of the South African government, now headed by Jan Christian Smuts, the Boer general defeated by the British in the Boer War.

Wealthy sympathizers of the penniless and homeless Satyagrahis established a huge farm outside Johannesburg to care for them. It was called Tolstoy Farm after the famed Russian author who preached nonviolence. There, Gandhi learned the crafts of weaving, carpentry, and leather working.

In 1914, South Africa, bowing to world opinion, the outrage of Great Britain itself, and the untiring leadership of Mohandas K. Gandhi, was ready to give in. Gandhi threatened to bring the government to its knees, with a march of thousands, if the cruel laws against Indians were not abolished immediately. South Africa, already locked in a paralyzing railway strike, could withstand no more conflict and passed the Indian Relief Act, putting an end to most of those laws.

Gandhi had won a great victory for racial equality and civil rights. "Democracy," he wrote, "is the finest thing in the world....He [General Smuts] started with being my bitterest opponent....Today he is my warmest friend."

In 1915, following the outbreak of World War I (1914-1918), Gandhi returned to India. Not all Indians welcomed him home, however. His ability to organize the people, and his vision of sacrifice and nonviolent civil disobedience made wealthy maharajas, well-connected businessmen, and the British nervous.

During this wartime period, some people thought that India should help Britain in return for more favorable conditions. Others wanted to revolt while England was busy fighting Germany. Gandhi insisted that India help England win the war. He felt that India would be rewarded with self-rule for this service.

Half a million Indians answered the call and fought alongside the British during the war. Yet India was not rewarded. Disappointed, Gandhi encouraged a movement for independence. In 1919, Great Britain passed censorship laws, banned freedom of assembly, and Gandhi's own writings. Gandhi and his followers refused to obey. Thousands were jailed. He called for a national nonviolent strike.

"Nonviolence," he preached, "is a weapon for the brave."

Despite Gandhi's call for peaceful protest, violence did occur. Three Englishmen died in riots at Amritsar. In a separate incident, fifteen thousand unarmed Amritsaris held an illegal meeting to protest the loss of their civil liberties. The British army fired on the crowd. Four hundred died. More than one thousand were wounded. Gandhi, outraged by the British action, decided to end his loyalty to the crown.

In 1920, nearly fifteen thousand delegates to the Indian National Congress voted for independence by peaceful means. Not all in India were comfortable with this position. Many upper-class Indians with British educations who owned property and had British pounds in their bank accounts saw their privileged futures at risk. But brushing aside these special interests, the great mass of Indians adopted Gandhi's ideas of satyagraha—truth and love—and refused to obey British colonial laws. Muslims and Hindus, who had previously fought against each other over religious differences, now joined together in loosening India from England.

Gandhi and his Muslim allies whipped up support for independence. Wherever Gandhi traveled, the common people fell at his feet, worshiping him as a divine messenger sent by God to free them. They began calling him mahatma ("Great Soul").

In 1921, fifty-two-year-old Mahatma Gandhi, now a weaver of home-spun cloth, began to wear nothing more than a poor man's loincloth, shawl, and sandals. With his simple manner, he stood as a symbol of India's anger over its colonial status. Gandhi's small body and tiny voice, no outward challenge to British power, were nevertheless recognized by millions of Indians as the essence of their nonviolent defiance of British authority.

Between 1922 and 1924 Gandhi was imprisoned for criticizing the British government. In 1930 he led a 241-mile march for salt, the poor family's staple, to protest the tax the British placed on it. Thousands of marchers were jailed. Nonviolent protest erupted nationwide. British police clubbed the protesters. No one struck back. "Nothing but organized nonviolence," wrote Gandhi, "can check the organized violence of the British government." Gandhi fasted to call the world's attention to India's plight.

With Britain occupied by World War II (1939–1945), Gandhi demanded independence. But, he said, "We do not seek our independence out of Britain's ruin." Described as a "half-naked seditionist" by a British official, Gandhi called for massive civil disobedience. He and many of his followers, including his wife, Kasturbai, were jailed for treason. With Gandhi imprisoned, there was no one to control the mob violence. The people rioted.

In 1946, a war-weary England proposed independence. But some Indian Muslims wanted their own country, and when the British left India on August 15, 1947, fighting, known as the Partition riots, broke out between the Muslims and the Hindus. Finally, Pakistan, a Muslim state, was carved out of West and East India. What remained of India in between would be Hindu.

Although the struggle for civil rights was far from over, Mahatma Gandhi's long fight for India's freedom had been won.

More About Gandhi

In 1948, Muslims fleeing Hindu India and Hindus fleeing Muslim Pakistan slaughtered each other. Gandhi pleaded for an end to the bloodshed. He fasted again to near death, proclaiming he would not eat until the warring factions would "forgive and forget." They did, happily, at his bedside.

Mahatma Gandhi's code of nonviolence and civil disobedience in the cause of social justice won him respect all over the world. He added a new, more moral dimension to humanity's constant quest for civil rights. Gandhi was gentle and generous with defeated adversaries. He forgave his enemies. But not all his enemies forgave him. In the end, Gandhi's nonviolent nature brought him violence.

Some Hindus were embittered by Gandhi's reconciliation with Muslims. They vowed to kill him. On January 30, 1948, one of them did, shooting Gandhi three times. Twenty years later, in 1968, the American civil rights leader the Reverend Dr. Martin Luther King Jr., having acknowledged Gandhi's principle of nonviolent protest as the basis for the U.S. civil rights movement of the late 1950s and 1960s, died of an assassin's bullet, too.

"It is nonviolence only when we love those that hate us," Gandhi had written before his death. "I know how difficult it is to follow this grand law of love. But are not all great and good things difficult to do? Love of the hater is the most difficult of all. But by the grace of God even this most difficult thing becomes easy to accomplish if we want to do it."

CHAPPAQUA LIBRARY

3 1005 15093713 6

J B GANDHI
Fisher, Leonard
Gandhi

CHAPPAQUA PUBLIC LIBRARY
CHAPPAQUA, NY 10514
914-238-4779